AS AN OAK TREE GROWS

G. Brian Karas

NANCY PAULSEN BOOKS ✇ AN IMPRINT OF PENGUIN GROUP (USA)

The author wishes to thank Martin Clarke and Charles Canham for their historical and scientific facts, the Town of Clinton Historical Society for sharing their vintage postcards, and Kimba and Christian Fekete for their wonderful old oak tree.

NANCY PAULSEN BOOKS
Published by the Penguin Group
Penguin Group (USA) LLC
375 Hudson Street, New York, NY 10014

USA | Canada | UK | Ireland | Australia
New Zealand | India | South Africa | China
penguin.com
A Penguin Random House Company

Library of Congress Cataloging-in-Publication Data
Karas, G. Brian, author, illustrator. As an oak tree grows / G. Brian Karas. pages cm
Summary: "From 1775 to the present, the landscape around a lone oak tree goes through significant changes" —Provided by publisher. [1. Oak—Fiction. 2. Trees—Fiction. 3. Growth—Fiction.] I. Title.
PZ7.K1296As 2014   [E]—dc23   2013036651

Manufactured in China by South China Printing Co. Ltd.
ISBN 978-0-399-25233-4
10 9 8 7 6 5 4 3 2 1

Design by Ryan Thomann. Text set in Maiandra Demi Bold.
The art was prepared with gouache and pencil.

In memory of Pete Seeger

On a sunny late summer day,
a young boy planted an acorn in the ground.

Later that year, an oak tree sprouted up from the earth, into the air and light.

1775

Each fall it will shed its leaves and
each spring new ones will grow.

The boy grew up and moved away. Farmers now lived here.
They cleared the hillsides where forests once stood.
The wood was used for building and to burn in fireplaces.

But the oak tree was left standing.

The oak tree had room to spread wide
and grew upward and outward.

Sometimes snow was very heavy
and a branch would break off.

As the oak tree grew, everyone and everything was on the move.
Children grew. Some stayed to work on the farms and others left to work
in factories. Ships came and went. Large engines rumbled along steel rails.

1775   1800   1825   1850

Birds perched in the oak tree to rest from long migrations.
Some stayed and made new homes, and others flew on.
More people arrived and built new houses and buildings.

Some years, little rain fell.
Hills and fields were dry where trees had once
stood and shaded the ground from the sun's rays.
The oak tree's roots reached far underground
for water as its leaves wilted.

Farmers conserved what little they had for thirsty livestock, until the rain fell again.

Electricity came through wires that were strung over hills and through valleys. It powered streetlamps and homes.

The land twinkled
with lights as stars
faded in the night sky.

1900

The oak tree grew slowly and steadily
while all around it life sped by.

People rode in cars to go to work
and visit friends, to go shopping
or just for a drive.

1900   1925

Soon the air was filled with
jet contrails, and radio waves,

and sound waves of beeping cars,
barking dogs, zooming motorboats,
whistling trains and music.

1900   1925   1950

The oak tree is two hundred years old. It has shed its leaves and grown new ones every year.

Animals, birds and insects have made homes
in its folds and holes and branches.

GASOLINE

1900   1925   1950   **1975**

The oak tree, with its strong roots, trunk and limbs,
has survived many storms over its lifetime.

Now a fog rolls in and a big storm is on the way.

The storm is powerful and the oak tree is
split in two. It does not survive this storm.

People come to look where the great oak tree once stood. The tree is cut into pieces to be used for furniture, firewood and mulch.

A new day dawns. Once again
the ground is warm and welcoming,
as a new oak tree grows.